MW01254295

For FJ, Ola & Oba

Once upon a time in a city not far from a hill,

there was a little farm that was as busy as could be.

It was home to many farm animals and was carefully managed by farmer Pete and his wife.

The cock was one of the animals on the farm and he was a very fine rooster.

He liked to believe that he owned the farm - well, next to farmer Pete of course.

He would perch on the fence, bright and early every morning and wake everyone else up with a very loud crow -

"Cock-a-doodle!"

"Get up everyone, what a mighty fine day it is today!"

One day, farmer Pete bought a new bull and brought it to the farm.

Everyone was quite happy to meet the new animal - everyone except the proud little rooster.

"Oh, a new farm animal" said the sheep,

"Welcome!!" chorused the ducklings,

"Look, he has a horn" said the cow;

"Humphh!" said the rooster with barely hidden disgust.

It was not long before the arguments started; The quarreling, the boasting and a lot of noise too.

Both Roosie the cock, and Billy the bull wanted to be the leader of the pack;

His Royal Highness, the king of the farm!

"My Dad had a horn like a unicorn" said the rooster,

"Well, my Grandpa could breathe out fire like a dragon and had dragon wings" replied the bull.

Not quite done with each other yet, they continued boasting.

"Sometimes I turn blue and grow wings" said the bull.

"Well, I could peck three corns in a row and turn into a pig" replied the cock.

A fairy perched on a nearby tree and listened to them boast.

She laughed so hard, she nearly fell. She decided to grant their wishes;

And so she waved her magic wand and their words came to life.

In the evening farmer Pete came to feed the animals;

Roosie gobbled up three grains in a row and what do you know?

He turned into a pig as pink as could be.

What do you suppose the farmer saw when he went to feed the cattle? A blue bull complete with long blue wings! He scratched his head.

He counted the cattle; One was missing and it was all blue!

Farmer Pete was so shocked to see strange animals on his farm.

So he shooed the weird pig out of his farm.

And called the doctor to check Billy the bull.

The doctor took a look at Billy and said there was nothing he could do.

Farmer Pete rang someone from the circus and sold the blue bull.

Now when Roosie left the farm, he ran down the road until he got to the city.

It was getting dark when he saw a little red building, so he walked through the doors right into a restaurant.

Everyone stopped and stared in horror as a pig strolled majestically into the restaurant.

"Look a pig!!" said a little boy pointing at the rooster.

"Excuse me,I'm a rooster" said Roosie proudly - but the problem was - he was squealing like a pig!

The cook came out with a knife and an evil gleam in his eyes.

Roosie fled the restaurant with the cook at his heels.

He ran so fast until he got to a circus where he saw a blue bull right there in the cage.

That must be Billy

"Billy...oh..Billy...I'm so glad to see you" said Roosie.

"Stay where you are, don't move closer" replied Billy grumpily.

" 'Tis I...the rooster"

The bull hung his head sadly; It was just his luck to end a very horrible day with a pig having some sort of problem understanding who he really was.

"Really it is" said Roosie "I turned into a pig this evening when farmer Pete came to feed everyone".

"Roosie? Is that really you?" asked Billy,

"Yes, you silly bull" replied Roosie;

And for the first time, they were truly happy to see each other.

"Let me out of here" said Billy.

The pig nudged the cage open with his head and they both tip-toed out of the circus.

"I'm sorry Billie,when I said I could turn into a pig, I was only lying" said Roosie.

"And when I said I could turn blue and grow wings,I was lying too" replied Billy.

They both sat in silence watching the stars in the sky.

Now the fairy just happened to be passing by and saw the two of them.

She felt sorry for them and knew they had learnt their lessons;

So she waved her magic wand and they both magically turned back into their normal selves.

They laughed and they cheered..

As they made their way back to Farmer Pete's farm.

"You can be the leader of the pack,if you want " said Roosie.

"No, you can be the leader if you want" replied Billy.

When Farmer Pete woke up to feed the animals the next day, the cock was right there and when he counted his cattle; Well, they were complete because the bull was there too!

He scratched his head, trying to figure it all out.

"Well, strange things seems to be happening on this farm" he muttered, as he walked back to the house to tell his wife all about it!

32435497R00017

Made in the USA
Lexington, KY
02 March 2019